All My Little Ducklings

All My Little Ducklings
Monica Wellington

E. P. DUTTON · NEW YORK

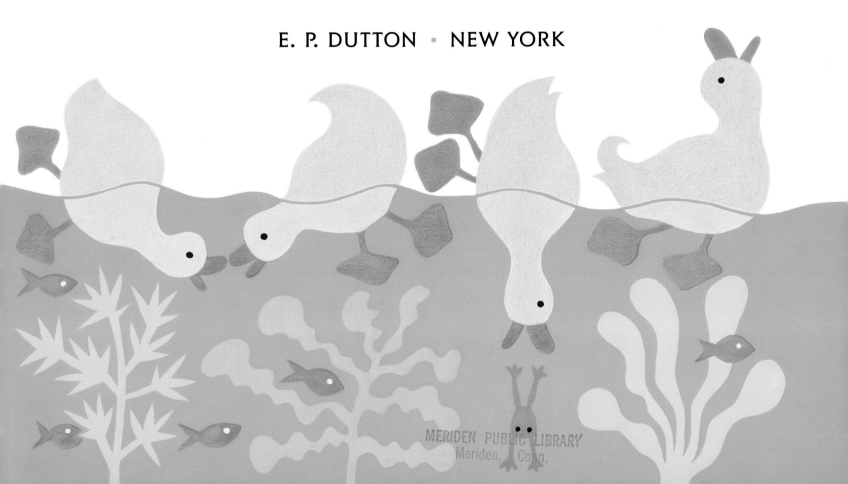

for Rhona Clement

Library of Congress Cataloging-in-Publication Data
Wellington, Monica.
  All my little ducklings / Monica Wellington.—Ist ed.
    p.   cm.
  Summary: Brief text and illustrations follow the activ-
ities of a group of ducklings in the water and on the shore.
  ISBN 0-525-44459-9
  [I. Ducks—Fiction.]   I. Title.   88-22841
PZ7.W4576AI   1989   CIP
[E]—dc19   AC

Published in the United States by E. P. Dutton,
2 Park Avenue, New York, N.Y. 10016,
a division of NAL Penguin Inc.

Published simultaneously in Canada by
Fitzhenry & Whiteside Limited, Toronto

Designer: Alice Lee Groton

Printed in Hong Kong by South China Printing Co.
First Edition   10 9 8 7 6 5 4 3 2 1

All my little ducklings
Waking with the light

Twisting Swishing
Flapping feet

Wiggle   Wiggle   Waggle

All my little ducklings
Waddle to the water

Flipping   Dipping   Splatter

Splash

Paddle in the pond

Heads are in the water
Tails are to the sun

Topsy-turvy Upside-down
Dibble Dibble Dabble

All my little ducklings

Paddling to the shore

Skimming Swimming

Picking Plucking
Nibble Nibble Munch

Go my little ducklings

Wander

Wonder

Ramble

Roam

Peeping Squeaking
Cackle Quack

Ducklings by the barn

Ducklings in the orchard

Chased by buzzing bees

Wibble Wobble in the woods

Pitter   Patter   Scatter

Where are all my ducklings?
Scrambling to the pond

Hurry
Hurry

Quack
Quack

Plunk Plonk

Splish Splosh

Back for one more swim

All my little ducklings
Muddle through the reeds

Mumble

Stumble

Bump

Cuddle Nuzzle Snuggle
Sleeping in our nest